BREAD, ROSES AND DIGNITY

Also by Alexandria Blaelock

SHORT STORY COLLECTIONS
The Histories of Hayward Hall
Lovelorn, Lovestruck and Love at First Sight
Common or Garden Variety Heroes
Case Files of the Wilkinson Detective Agency
Unavoidable Fates
Christmas Travesties
Five Faces of Felicia Clarke
Little Place Called Home
Security Directorate Dossiers v. 1.
Security Directorate Dossiers v. 2.

NOVELLAs
That Love Nonsense
Taipan vs Brown
The Ghost and Ms Cox
Friends Like That
Weaving the Wildwood
Wolf vs Orb

MS BLAELOCK'S BOOKS
Stress Free Dinner Parties
Signature Wardrobe Planning
Holistic Personal Finance
Minimally Viable Housekeeping
Planning a Life Worth Living

PICTURE BOOKS
Australia Felix

SELECTED SHORT STORIES
Alma's Grace
Blood and Bloody Profanity
Cancelled by the Cartel
Dingo Hunting
Honoris Virilis Respectu
Mince Pie Mystery
Remains of Christmas

BREAD, ROSES AND DIGNITY

ALEXANDRIA BLAELOCK

BlueMere Books

MELBOURNE, AUSTRALIA

Publisher's Note: This is a work of fiction. Names, characters, places, and incidents are a product of the author's imagination. Locations and public names are sometimes used for atmosphere. Any resemblance to actual people, living or dead, or to businesses, companies, events, institutions, or locations is completely coincidental.

Copyright © 2025 by Alexandria Blaelock.

All rights reserved. No part of this book may be used or reproduced directly, or through text or data mining, to train artificial intelligence technologies or systems. Neither may it be reproduced, distributed or transmitted in any form or by any means, including photocopying, recording, or other electronic or mechanical methods, without the prior written permission of the publisher, except in the case of brief quotations embodied in critical reviews and certain other non-commercial uses permitted by copyright law.

For permission requests, please contact enquiries@bluemerebooks.com.

Ordering Information:
Discounts are available on quantity purchases. For details, contact orders@bluemerebooks.com.

Bread, Roses and Dignity/Alexandria Blaelock
paperback ISBN: 978-1-923083-29-5
digital ISBN: 978-1-923083-30-1

Book Layout © BookDesignTemplates.com
Cover Art © Ole Schwander/Depositphotos

BREAD, ROSES AND DIGNITY

The day was bitterly cold, and all Pearl could see around her was grey. Grey sky, grey buildings, and the grey faced inhabitants of Lawrence, Massachusetts.

The frozen snow her boots crunched over was grey, tainted with wood ash, coal dust and horse shit, but at least it didn't smell right now.

Mind you, it was hard to know whether the mass of people congregating outside the mill contributed more to the stench that the shit. It was just enough to cover the hint of woodsmoke from cooking fires.

Pearl absently rubbed her thumb over the slowly healing stub of her middle finger. The one the new loom had taken the tip off when she was too slow to get her hand out of the way.

She was lucky though; her brother Charles broke his leg in three places when they were installing and testing the new machines. He'd never walk without a crutch again.

And he lost his job at the mill because he couldn't keep up with the machine. Laid off with barely a thank you, let alone any money towards his medical care. And that wasn't cheap.

He was still so low about how it took him such a long time to get down the four flights of tenement stairs to the toilets.

Just as well the queues were so long, because he was in so much pain he needed to rest when he got down.

And then a rest before he started the climb back up, a rest half way, and another when he arrived back at their room.

Hopefully he'd feel better soon, and get to the point where he could get out there to make some money and contribute.

At the moment he was a massive drain on the family economy.

And every night when she got back from the picket, she found him more and more down.

It was beginning to feel like he wasn't ever going to pull himself together, like it was only a matter of time before he just gave up and died.

It was kinda nice how the other folks in the tenement kept an eye out for him, but their patience was bound to wear thin soon enough.

What with the cramped conditions, lack of sanitation and good food, it wasn't as it he had it that much harder than everyone else.

It seemed like every other day someone woke up dead and the word went through the tenement that someone else needed money for another funeral.

If there's no money coming in, then there's no money for the life insurance either.

They all did their best to help each out where they could.

Life might be cheap, but death sure was not.

And so many of them were dying too young, in cramped, overcrowded and under heated tenements.

Like when Pa died after being crushed at the mill and Ma had gone mad.

Who knows what would have happened if the neighbours hadn't stepped in and taken care of everything.

Indirectly, that's how Pearl, Ma and her five younger siblings came to share a room with two other families - twelve people crammed into one tiny room.

Lucky there was a good mix of night and day workers. Imagine if all of them were trying to sleep at night.

Mind you, the amount of fights that broke out over who was cooking over the fire, and who stole whose bucket of water had to be seen to believed.

The luxury of a room of her own was way out of her grasp, but a room for just the family was something they could achieve if they all pulled together.

And maybe a decent meal now and again with meat and fresh vegetables, not just stale bread with stews made of dried beans.

Lord knows working fifty-six hours a week at the mill was a bad enough way to earn $8.76. Not that anyone only worked fifty-six hours. Sixty-hour weeks were more often the minimum.

The builders, miners and printers had won eight-hour days, yet weavers were still struggling along on ten-hour days six days a week.

Some working even longer.

So, cutting back to fifty-four-hour weeks was seen as a good thing right up until everyone realised they'd lost thirty two cents in the deal.

That was it, "short pay, all out," and out they'd gone.

Snowflakes stung her face as she looked around for George, nodding to people she knew from the mill or had come to know during the picketing.

Pearl pulled her well-used threadbare coat closer around her and stamped her feet to try to warm her frozen toes.

At least her legs were a little warmer now she'd patched her skirt with the remains of one owned by a dead woman she'd bought when someone'd come looking for funeral money.

The strike had been long and difficult, but they were still resolute. They weren't going back until they'd got a fifteen percent pay increase for the fifty-four-hour week, double pay for overtime, and the abolition of the premium and bonus systems.

Not to mention an agreement not to discriminate against the strikers.

Mr Ettor from the Industrial Workers of the World and that Italian Socialist Mr Giovanitti had formed a committee, and they were going to make it happen.

They'd managed to unite all the workers from all the Lawrence mills together to picket in the interests of all, so who knew what they might achieve.

That had to be so much better than taking the mills on one by one like the American Federation of Labor wanted.

All for one and all that.

You had to wonder at times, who these people were looking out for.

Them and the United Textile Workers.

You didn't even know what they were talking about half the time because they only spoke English and didn't bother to get any translators in at their meetings.

They probably never even bothered to ask what the mill workers wanted.

The mill owners had turned the fire hoses on the picketers, and then called the police when the picketers had thrown the ice back.

Then that mill-owning SOB Governor Foss had called out the state militia and the state police to reinforce the local forces.

Pearl wasn't sure she'd ever forget the day they'd shot Anna LoPizzo.

They'd been peaceably walking the mills when the police cordon had closed in, trapping them in the centre. When it had got so tight they could hardly move, the police pulled out their clubs and started beating picketers right, left and centre.

Obviously people had tried to fight their way free, they were afraid for their lives!

But that didn't mean the police had to get their guns out and start shooting people.

And if that wasn't enough, the Governor's militia had bayoneted young John Ramey who was just playing his trumpet.

Naturally they said he'd backed into them: they weren't going to admit they'd charged unarmed people in their own town, were they?

Who knows what that Colonel Sweetser was thinking ordering them out with bayonet's charged?

It's not like they were Mexicans or Indians intent on rebellion or murder or anything.

She'd met George during one of the early police attacks. He'd sheltered her with his body as the police had laid about with their clubs.

She'd been shocked that he'd dared to touch her so intimately, but had appreciated his courage.

And his body warmth.

She'd been worried about him, and after that had looked for him every time the pickets reassembled.

It had taken several days, but she'd found him eventually.

He was battered and bruised, but no broken bones.

"Fighting fit," he claimed.

After that, they'd sought each other out, day after day, and over the last few weeks their friendship had grown closer and love had blossomed.

They'd dared to start talking of a time after the strike.

When they could overcome their family's racial prejudices and maybe marry.

They were two ordinary working people, just like all the others massing every day.

Peacefully protesting, asking for not just bread, but roses too.

Not just a decent standard of living with good food to eat, but dignity too.

The opportunity to access art and music, to develop skills and live a full and meaningful life.

Maybe the current combined suffering of the mill worker communities could overcome their historic racial differences to forge a new tolerance for each other too.

What with all the violence and the arrests of Ettor and Giovanitti, was it any wonder people wanted to send their kids away to safety?

So why were the police sent to arrest them at the train station?

How is it lawful to arrest someone for sending their child to visit someone in another city?

And how is it lawful to pull out a club and lay into them when they try.

Not only the adults but the children too?

Enough so as Mrs Bextris or whatever her name was miscarried.

And then she, and the other women were sent to prison the very same day for not paying their arrest fines!

In this day and age, how is all that possible?

They might as well have stayed back in their old countries as come here.

All of this for thirty-two cents a week? Though that's three loaves of bread, and you got to eat.

Especially when Lawrence is one of the most congested and expensive places to live in the entire country.

How can one man employ hundreds of people, yet not give a hoot about them?

Like they's just a different kind of machine to the new coal fired looms.

Mind you, beating up women and children had attracted Mrs Taft's interest, and it seemed like she'd spoken to the President because there was going to be an inquiry.

The mockery of running a loom producing some of the finest wool cloth in the country wasn't lost on Pearl.

That those soldiers doing the Governor's bidding were probably wearing fabric made in her mill.

That maybe Mrs Taft had bought a coat made from Lawrence cloth worth ten whole dollars from Bloomingdale's. More likely had one made for maybe forty dollars or more.

All happening when she and the other workers barely made enough to feed and house their families.

It was nigh on unendurable.

She'd been nearly nine weeks on strike so far. Thank goodness the IWW had called for support from other textile towns.

They'd raised funds to provide strikers with a little money to keep them going, set up soup kitchens and free medical care to help ease the burden.

She and the other picketers couldn't have survived without them.

Something had to be done.

And Pearl was going to keep standing out here, and marching around the town in one of the coldest winters on record until something was done about it.

No matter how long it took.

Strong arms grabbed her from behind, and she started struggling to free herself until she heard George's voice behind her, "there you are! I've been looking for you for ages."

She turned and looked up into his square, clean-shaven face, his sparkling blue eyes looking back at her.

Pearl swatted his arm, "you scared me."

He grinned, picked her up and twirled her in a circle, "did you hear? They gave in. The strike's over!"

"It's over? We won?"

"It's definitely over, and we definitely won."

She hugged him, and not caring what anyone thought, she kissed him too.

They held each other's hands and jumped for joy. The beatings, cold and suffering had all been worth it.

And if the community could pull together to achieve this, who knew what they could do in the future.

All around her the murmur of happy people spreading the news increased to a roar.

They were hugging each other, dancing as they laughed and cried. Here and there someone burst into song, and more and more people joined in.

Thousands of voices in dozens of languages, all celebrating the victory of the many poor over the rich few.

THE END

AUTHOR'S NOTE

This story is a fictional retelling of what has come to be known as the Bread and Roses Strike of 1912 in Lawrence Massachusetts.

People really did die during the strike. Women and children were beaten up.

Police and soldiers were brought in to break it up, and as hard as it is for us to imagine, bayonets and bullets were used.

Yet, the millworkers, caught between a rock and a hard place, stood firm together.

For as long as I can remember, I've been of the opinion that a fair day's work should earn you a fair day's pay.

That all people who perform the same job should earn the same wage regardless of age or gender, though I warrant that someone who's been in the job longer might be entitled to higher wages given they have more experience..

I also think a fair day's pay should net you a wage you can actually live off, because I am well aware that while many employers are happy to make profits, they're less happy about sharing them with the people who make them possible.

Or worse, steal their entitlements.

If you can't afford to pay your employees properly, you shouldn't be in business.

And as far as I'm concerned, working for tips, is criminal.

That being the case, I'm grateful for the people who made my opinion possible, and I'm proud to live in one of the cities that made the eight hour day possible.

> Eight hours to work,
> Eight hours to play,
> Eight hours to sleep,
> Eight bob a day.
> A fair day's work,
> For a fair day's pay.
>
> Worker's Ditty

Though it took a long time...

The conditions those long dead workers fought for are largely gone now.

Modern work more often consists of casual, gigs (the modern equivalent of piece work), short-term contracts, and more often that not, here today and gone tomorrow.

Yet, for some lucky ones, there's more flexibility; working from home, structuring your work week to suit your life and cultural beliefs, and the opportunity to cut your commute times.

Ways of working unthinkable not long ago!

But I hope people are choosing to manage their work and their lives, rather than having their choices taken away.

And if they aren't, I hope they find like minded people to work together with to change the future of work for the better.

Alexandria Blaelock
Melbourne
2025

As a small token of my thanks for reading...

Please enjoy 10% off everything (excluding shipping)

at alexandriablaelock.com

with the code pearlten.

Turn the page for some ideas where to use it,

IF YOU ENJOYED THIS STORY,

you might like these books

Felicia Clarke; influencer.
Old Fashioned. Fiercely independent.
Encourages others, but treads her own path.
Dead, but fondly remembered.
By some.
Get to know Felicaia through these five stories.

Common or Garden Variety Heroes

Do you have what it takes to be a hero?

Whether that's running into a burning building, standing up for what you know is right, or saving the Princess it's going to take everything you've got and more besides.

In this genre-spanning collection of original stories, five women draw on resources they didn't know they had.

Join them, if you dare.

The Histories of Hayward Hall

Meet Morag Clementine. The new housekeeper at historic Hayward Hall.

Her practical and capable attitude usually keeps her out of trouble.

Above all, her no-nonsense, get it done approach. And her get in the middle of the scrum outlook.

Just as well, because Hayward Hall needs someone like her.

Little Place Called Home

Home is where the heart is.

You can struggle to find the place you call home.

It's not a place, it's a feeling. You'll know it when you find it.

This collection of short stories explores our search for a place we can call home.

Short, sweet and relatable, these stories will make you homesick for places you've never been.

Perhaps you'll carry your new books
in one of these bags

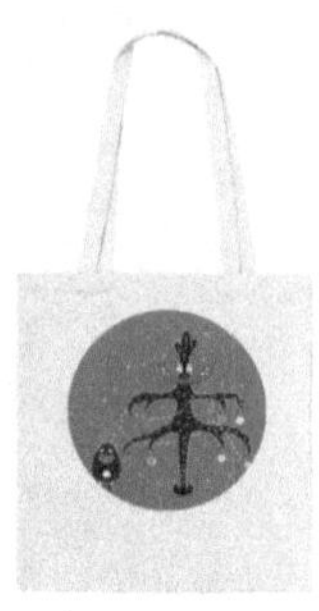

And enjoy them while you're drinking
from one of these mugs

ABOUT THE AUTHOR

Australian author Alexandria Blaelock writes mostly fantasy and mystery.

She's appeared in the Stringybark Anthology *Crowd Surfing*, *Pulphouse Fiction Magazine*, and *Ellery Queen's Mystery Magazine*.

She's also written five self-help books applying business techniques to personal matters like getting dressed, tidying up, and feeding friends.

Discover more at https://alexandriablaelock.com.

www.ingramcontent.com/pod-product-compliance
Lightning Source LLC
Chambersburg PA
CBHW051830180726
48283CB00004BA/1376